Seniors of t

A Comedy in Two

by Barbara Pease Weber

Baker's Plays
7611 Sunset Blvd.
Los Angeles, CA 90042
bakersplays.com

NOTICE

This book is offered for sale at the price quoted only on the understanding that, if any additional copies of the whole or any part are necessary for its production, such additional copies will be purchased. The attention of all purchasers is directed to the following: This work is protected under the copyright laws of the United States of America, in the British Empire, including the Dominion of Canada, and all other countries adhering to the Universal Copyright Convention. Violations of the Copyright Law are punishable by fine or imprisonment, or both. The copying or duplication of this work or any part of this work, by hand or by any process, is an infringement of the copyright and will be vigorously prosecuted.

This play may not be produced by amateurs or professionals for public or private performance without first submitting application for performing rights. Royalties are due on all performances whether for charity or gain, or whether admission is charged or not. Since performance of this play without the payment of the royalty fee renders anybody participating liable to severe penalties imposed by the law, anybody acting in this play should be sure, before doing so, that the royalty fee has been paid. Professional rights, reading rights, radio broadcasting, television and all mechanical rights, etc. are strictly reserved. Application for performing rights should be made directly to BAKER'S PLAYS.

No one shall commit or authorize any act or omission by which the copyright of, or the right to copyright, this play may be impaired. No one shall make any changes in this play for the purpose of production.

Publication of this play does not imply availability for performance. Both amateurs and professionals considering a production are strongly advised in their own interest to apply to Baker's Plays for written permission before starting rehearsals, advertising, or booking a theatre.

Whenever the play is produced, the author's name must be carried in all publicity, advertising and programs. Also, the following notice must appear on all printed programs, "Produced by special arrangement with Baker's Plays."

Licensing fees for *SENIORS OF THE SAHARA* is based on a per performance rate and payable one week in advance of the production.

Please consult the Baker's Plays website at www.bakersplays.com or our current print catalogue for up to date licensing fee information.

CHARACTERS

(In order of appearance)

REFIK* – An unlucky merchant at an outdoor market.

SAVALAS** – Eugene's former master. The bad guy.

FANNIE GREEN – One of Sylvia Goldberg's best friends. Wait till you see her belly dance!

MABEL MILLSTEIN – Sylvie's very best friend. (A real yenta.)

THELMA WACHTER – Another of Sylvie's best friends. (Just don't let her drive at night.)

SYLVIA GOLDBERG – A respectable retired school teacher from Margate, New Jersey.

EUGENE – A geriatric genie with a bad back and a penchant for vodka and V8.

HERMAN* – Mabel's cousin from Long Branch. Not such a bad guy after all.

MASTER OF CEREMONIES – (can be acted on stage or off stage)

*Refik and Herman may be portrayed by the same actor.

**If necessary, Savalas and Master of Ceremonies may be portrayed by the same actor.

SENIORS OF THE SAHARA was featured in September 2007 at the McLaren Comedy Play Festival in Midland, Texas and simultaneously premiered at The Old Academy in Philadelphia, Pennsylvania. Nancy Frick produced The Old Academy production with the following cast:

REFIK/HERMAN.................................Peter Javsicas

SAVALAS ....Paul Muscarella

FANNIE GREEN............................... Theresa Bateman

MABEL MILLSTEIN............................. Susan Lonker

THELMA WACHTER .... J. J. Johnson

SYLVIA GOLDBERG ....Joanne Brecht

EUGENE ....Alan Packer/ J. P. Parrella

MASTER OF CEREMONIES . . . John Paul Weber/George E. Beetham, Jr.

for John,
then, now, always

ACT I

(PRE-CURTAIN: The following "Prequel" may be performed live in front of the audience, live in silhouette or pre-recorded. If performed live before an audience it must be done in such a way to prevent **REFIK** *from actually being smacked or hurt. In any event, the scene is to be performed to give the impression that* **REFIK** *and* **SAVALAS** *are in a "far off land.")*

(Exotic music is heard such as a flute and a drum to suggest that a snake is being charmed somewhere in the distance. As the music fades, an audible SLAP is followed by a groan of pain.)

REFIK. No, no more. Stop. Savalas, please! I beg you.

SAVALAS. How could you be so *stupid.* You fool! *(another audible SLAP)*

REFIK. OWWWW. Stop, please, it was an accident. I swear to you.

SAVALAS. Accident! HA! How much did they pay you, Refik? How much gold did you receive to part with it? *(SLAP)*

REFIK. Savalas, you must believe me. I did not sell for profit. I make no money.

SAVALAS. I don't believe you. *(SLAP, SLAP)*

REFIK. Owwwww. *(begging)* Please don't kill me. I have a wife, a child, a goat, a parakeet! *(SLAP)* Owww.

SAVALAS. They are of no concern to me. If you do not return the treasure, you will all die. Now, *where* is it? This is the last time I will ask.

REFIK. I do not know. A woman purchased it. An *old* woman.

SAVALAS. You're lying, Refik. If you don't start telling me the truth I will…. *(SLAP)*

REFIK. Owww. It's true. I swear on my great grandfather's tomb. It was sold to the old lady by accident.

SAVALAS. How can it be an "accident" to relinquish such rare and powerful treasure to an old woman! You *lie*. *(SLAP)*

REFIK. No, I did not. My wife! By accident, she sold it. When I went home to walk the goat. I was only gone for 10 minutes. She did not know the difference. My wife make a mistake. She has no idea of the treasure hidden inside. She just think she make a regular transaction. They all look the same to her. Cheap imitations of archaeological relics. *(SLAP)* OWWWW. This is the truth, Savalas. You must believe me.

SAVALAS. And you say an "old woman" bought the treasure. Who is she?

REFIK. She is an American tourist. A senior citizen!

SAVALAS. An elderly American tourist? I do not think so! Do not continue to lie to me, Refik, or your lies will be the last words you speak! *(SLAP)*

REFIK. I'm not lying to you, Savalas I can prove it!

SAVALAS. How?

REFIK. I have a receipt! A credit card receipt. American Express!

SAVALAS. Let me see it. *(SLAP)*

REFIK. Owww, stop please. Here. Here it is.

*(**REFIK** hands the receipt to **SAVALAS**.)*

SAVALAS. *(reads receipt)* Receipt of sale. Sold to *Sylvia Goldberg*? Your wife sold this treasure to *Sylvia Goldberg* for thirty dollars! THIRTY DOLLARS! The rarest and most valuable treasure in the entire world and your foolish wife sells it to an elderly Jewish woman for THIRTY DOLLARS!! *(SLAP, SLAP, SLAP)* This is your fault. You should not have put it among your merchandise.

REFIK. Owwww! I am sorry. I thought it would blend in without notice. I thought to hide it in plain sight. I now know it was a bad idea. *(SLAP)* Agghh!

SAVALAS. And where does this woman live? How do you know she is American? She could be Israeli. She could be British. What am I to do? Should I telephone American Express and ask "Hello, may I have the address of one of your customers? An old woman by the name of Sylvia Goldberg." *(SLAP)*

REFIK. My wife, she asked the woman for identification. I have the Passport information.

SAVALAS. Give it to me! *(SLAP)*

*(**REFIK** hands the additional information to **SAVALAS**.)*

REFIK. Here. Please, no more torture, I beg you.

SAVALAS. Sylvia Goldberg, Number 302, The Gardens on Jerome, Margate, New Jersey. *NEW JERSEY????*

*(SLAP SLAP SLAP/**REFIK** GROANS IN PAIN)*

Of all of the places in the world, your stupid cow of a wife sells a priceless relic to an elderly Jewish woman from *Margate, New Jersey*! There's only one thing left for me to do.

REFIK. Please don't kill me!

SAVALAS. *I must find her!*

(BLACKOUT)

*(Exotic music once again plays as **SAVALAS** and **REFIK** exit the stage.)*

(CURTAIN OPENS/LIGHTS UP)

(SETTING: Sylvia Goldberg's condominium in Margate, New Jersey.)

(AT RISE: **MABEL MILLSTEIN** *and* **FANNIE GREEN** *are decorating* **SYLVIE***'s condo with balloons and signs "Welcome Home Sylvie."* **SYLVIE** *is about to return from three weeks in Israel where her grandson has just gotten married.)*

FANNIE. I'm wondering if we should be doing this, Mabel. She'll probably have jet lag.

MABEL. Sylvie's the only one I know who can sleep better on an airplane than in her own bed. She'll get home and want to stay up and talk all night. You know, the time difference and all.

FANNIE. I hope you're right. But, if she looks too tired we shouldn't stay long.

MABEL. Hand me the tape.

*(***MABEL*** climbs on a chair to tape the sign to the wall.)*

FANNIE. You be careful! If you fall off that chair you'll break a hip or worse.

MABEL. Quit worrying over me. I've got more padding than a football player. Now, give me the tape. We don't have much time.

*(***FANNIE*** hand her the tape and ***MABEL*** tapes the sign.)*

FANNIE. I don't know if I like this idea, yelling "*Surprise*" and all. We just may scare her into a heart attack.

MABEL. You worry too much. She'll love all of the attention. Besides, I missed her while she was gone.

FANNIE. Gee, thanks a lot.

MABEL. Oh, come on. You did too!

FANNIE. Of course I did. Three weeks is a long time for Sylvie to be away! But, I enjoyed spending the time with you.

MABEL. And I liked your company too, Fannie. It's just, well, you know, Sylvie's like the glue that holds us old gals together.

FANNIE. I can't wait to see her! I want to hear all about Barry's wedding. It's such an honor to be the grandmother of the groom. And, with the wedding in Israel, Sylvie had the trip of a lifetime!

MABEL. She certainly did. And she'll never admit it but I always thought that Barry was her favorite grandchild. *(inspecting the house plants)* Fannie, you did a nice job of watering Sylvie's plants while she was away.

FANNIE. *(proudly)* I did, didn't I? And you did a good job too picking up her mail each day from the box.

MABEL. What are friends for?

(The phone rings three times. MABEL moves to answer phone but FANNIE holds her back and listens for the rings.)

FANNIE. That's Thelma's signal. She's watching out the window for Sylvie's taxi.

MABEL. Is she coming down?

FANNIE. Yes, as soon as she gave us the signal.

MABEL. Why did she have to give a signal? We could have answered the phone.

FANNIE. I know. But a signal is more fun.

MABEL. Someone should have picked up Sylvie at the airport.

FANNIE. We don't drive anymore!

MABEL. Thelma still drives.

FANNIE. Not at night. Not anymore.

MABEL. Since when?

FANNIE. Since she ran over Rhoda Bennett's cat.

MABEL. She did? Did she kill it?

FANNIE. Dead as a doornail. You were down in Florida with Trudy Schoeman it happened.

MABEL. So why didn't you tell me when I got back?

FANNIE. Because Thelma feels so terrible about it. That's why she stopped driving at night.

MABEL. Rhoda loved her pussycat!

FANNIE. It was dark outside. Thelma didn't see it.

MABEL. She doesn't blame Thelma does she? After all, Rhoda's cat was pure black.

FANNIE. Thelma ran over the white one.

MABEL. Oy.

FANNIE. Anyway, that's when Thelma stopped driving at night.

MABEL. Well, it's hardly Thelma's fault if Rhoda's cat ran in front of her car.

FANNIE. Snowball was sleeping on the front porch. Thelma misjudged the driveway.

(knock at the door)

FANNIE & MABEL. Thelma!

*(**MABEL** goes to the door and opens it.)*

MABEL. Hurry! Come on in.

*(**THELMA WACHTER** enters carrying a home made cake.)*

THELMA. Did you get my signal?

MABEL. Loud and clear.

THELMA. I was keeping watch out the front window . I got so nervous when I saw Sylvie's taxi pull up that I called the wrong number at first. I think I dialed Mr. Feldman in 412. *(holding out the cake)* I baked Sylvie a welcome home cake!

(She puts it on the kitchen counter.)

FANNIE. I forgot to put the coffee on!

(She runs into the kitchen.)

MABEL. Not now! Wait until when she gets here. Turn off the lights. Now let's hide!

THELMA. This is so exciting! I love surprises!

FANNIE. Me too!

(She turns off the lamp.)

MABEL. Fannie, you hide in the bathroom. I'll hide in the kitchen and Thelma, you hide in the hall closet.

*(They all retreat to their hiding spots. **MABEL** is crouched behind the kitchen counter/half wall.)*

(After a beat or two, **THELMA** *pokes her head out of the closet and whispers loudly.)*

THELMA. How will we know when to yell "*Surprise?*"

*(***MABEL***'s head pops up from behind the half wall.)*

MABEL. I didn't think of that. *(thinks)* Let's all hide in the kitchen! Quick!

*(***THELMA*** *goes into the kitchen and crouches behind the counter/half wall.* **MABEL** *goes to bathroom where* **FANNIE** *is hiding, knocks first, then opens door.)*

Change of plans. We all have to hide in the kitchen.

FANNIE. How come?

THELMA. *(peeping up from behind counter)* So we can know when to shout "Surprise."

FANNIE. Oh! Right!

(They all hide in the kitchen area behind the half- wall/ counter.)

FANNIE. Who's going to count to three?

MABEL. If we count first, she'll hear us.

THELMA. I'll give a signal then we'll all yell "*Surprise.*"

MABEL. We don't need a signal. When Sylvie turns on the lights, we'll jump up and yell "Surprise". Okay?

FANNIE & THELMA. *(concurrently)* Okay./Good idea.

(They get into position.)

FANNIE. Mabel?

MABEL. What?

FANNIE. My foot fell asleep. Can I say "*Surprise*" from down here?

(There is a noise at the front door.)

MABEL. Quiet! Here she comes.

(The door opens and **SAVALAS** *enters dressed as a pizza delivery man carrying a small flashlight [turned on] and pizza box. He puts down the pizza box on the coffee table. Since the lights did not go on,* **THELMA, MABEL** *and* **FANNIE** *do not yell "Surprise."* **SAVALAS** *searches the*

living room, does not find what he is looking for, then goes into the bedroom to search. After he exits into the bedroom, **FANNIE, THELMA** *and* **MABEL** *"stage whisper" amongst themselves from the crouching position behind the kitchen side of the half wall/counter.)*

FANNIE. She didn't turn on the lights.

THELMA. Maybe she's trying to save on her electric bill.

MABEL. She probably had to go to the bathroom.

THELMA. Do you smell pizza?

FANNIE. When should we say *"Surprise?"*

MABEL. When she turns on the light.

FANNIE. What if she doesn't turn it on?

THELMA. When she comes back, I'll tap your shoulders then well yell *"Surprise"* if she doesn't turn on the light. That'll be the signal.

FANNIE. Do you think she went straight to bed?

THELMA. Maybe she's sick!

MABEL. Let's give her a minute. All right?

FANNIE & THELMA. *(concurrently)* All right/Okay.

(Shuffling noises are heard from the bedroom.)

MABEL. Shhh. She's coming back.

(In another few seconds, **SAVALAS** *returns quietly and continues searching the living room. He goes to the window and pulls the curtains closed. Then he turns on the light. The ladies jump up and yell "SURPRISE."* **SAVALAS** *screams a panic scream,* **FANNIE, THELMA** *and* **MABEL** *scream in reply and* **SAVALAS** *runs out the front door. A few moments later, in all of the commotion,* **SYLVIE** *enters.)*

SYLVIE. What in the world is going on in here? And, what did you do to the pizza man?

MABEL, THELMA & FANNIE. *(half heartedly)* Surprise.

(BLACKOUT)

(Later that evening. The police have come to take a report from the ladies who are recovering from the "Surprise" intruder. Sylvie's suitcases have been delivered to

her apartment by the doorman. The pizza box has been removed by the police. Fannie has made coffee and there are cups on the coffee table. MABEL *and* SYLVIE *are in the hallway by the front door saying goodbye to the police officers who have just left.)*

SYLVIE. *(from doorway into the hall)* Thank you again for coming so quickly officers. Good night.

MABEL. *(calling down the hall after the officers)* Officer Schnieder, don't forget now! My youngest granddaughter, Bonnie, is working over in Ocean City for the summer. At the Beach Grille. Bonnie Edelman. She doesn't work Mondays so don't go then. You two would make such a nice couple! Remember, Bonnie Edelman. She's *very* pretty! *(She enters the apartment.)* What a nice young man!

SYLVIE. *(locking the door)* Well, you gals certainly know how to throw a homecoming party! Oh shoot. In all the commotion I forgot to tip Sonny for bringing up my bags.

MABEL. That nice young officer is so smart! He told me he's starting law school in August. He'd be just perfect for Bonnie. You know, it all makes perfect sense. Everything he said.

FANNIE. What makes sense?

MABEL. That burglars disguise themselves as delivery men to get into buildings like this. He said that the burglar probably just came in through beach entrance with people who were either coming in or going out.

THELMA. Sure. Who would question a pizza delivery?

SYLVIE. But do burglars buy real pizzas before they rob a place? Wouldn't they use an empty pizza box?

THELMA. Maybe they use a real pizza so it looks more authentic if a security guard stops them.

MABEL. That makes sense.

FANNIE. Why did the police take the pizza away? I'm hungry.

MABEL. They had to. It's evidence.

THELMA. It is?

MABEL. They can test in their crime lab. I saw it on the television. *Law and Order* I think.

FANNIE. I bet they ate it.

THELMA. What if it's poison? What if robbers poison the pizza and make their victims eat it!

MABEL. Yes! I saw that on a *CSI* episode.

FANNIE. In that case I'm glad I didn't eat any. Can we cut your cake now, Thelma?

THELMA. Of course. Sylvie, I baked you a welcome home cake!

(She gets the cake from the kitchen.)

SYLVIE. Thank you, Thelma. That was very sweet of you.

MABEL. I think they'll probably try to find out which pizza place it came from. Then they'll try to figure out who bought it. They have special detectives, like Jerry Orbach on *Law and Order,* who do that you know. He's my favorite of all of the TV detectives.

THELMA. The other policeman, the older fellow, he told me that we shouldn't tell people when we go away on vacation. Burglars rob people who are away because it's easier to sneak in and out without getting caught.

MABEL. I didn't pay much attention him. He had on a wedding ring.

THELMA. What are you talking about?

MABEL. The older policeman with the brown hair had on a wedding ring. Too bad. He seems to be the perfect age for Rhoda's daughter. You know, the one who just got divorced. Otherwise, I would have mentioned her to him.

FANNIE. I think half the people in South Jersey knew about Barry getting married in Israel. You've been talking about it for months, Sylvie.

SYLVIE. So did you when your Amy got married. I'm not going to keep my grandson's wedding a secret! How did I know I'd get robbed – or – almost robbed. I'm just relieved that he didn't hurt any of you. He didn't have a gun or a knife did he? What if he had started shooting?

FANNIE. I didn't see. I got stuck on the floor and couldn't get up. I just screamed because Thelma and Mabel screamed.

MABEL. I think we really caught him off guard. He just screamed when we all shouted "*SURPRISE*" and then he ran out the door.

SYLVIE. Thank goodness no one was hurt!

MABEL. Well, Sylvie, I'm sorry your Surprise Party was a bust. I'm going upstairs to lock all my doors and windows and go to bed. Not that I'll sleep a wink, mind you.

FANNIE. Have your cake first. This is good Thelma! Very moist.

THELMA. Thanks. It's got instant pudding in it, that's why.

MABEL. *(eating the cake, to* **THELMA***)* You're not having any? What's wrong?

THELMA. Oh, I'm afraid to go home now.

FANNIE. So am I.

MABEL. The officers checked each floor. The robber is long gone. The police may have even caught him by now. *(referring to cake)* This *is* good.

THELMA. We sure scared him away, didn't we!

FANNIE. We sure did! That'll teach him to think twice before trying to rob old ladies.

SYLVIE. Before you go, since you went to all this trouble to throw me a welcome home party, let me at least give you your gifts.

FANNIE. *(gleefully)* You got us presents?

SYLVIE. Of course I did! Now just a minute, let me think where I put them.

(She opens up her suitcase and routes around a little.)

SYLVIE. *(cont.)* Here they are.

(She removes three packages and gives the first to **FANNIE.***)*

Fannie, this is a little something to thank you for watering my plants while I was away.

(She hands **FANNIE** *her gift.)*

FANNIE. Thank you **SYLVIE.**

(She opens the gift – a silk scarf –)

Oh, it's beautiful. I love it. You know how I love scarves.

(She puts it on.)

SYLVIE. I got it in Tel Aviv. It's pure silk.

MABEL. It looks nice on you Fannie.

SYLVIE. Mabel, thank you for checking my mailbox each day. Oh, did my package from QVC come?

MABEL. Yes, it's in your bedroom.

SYLVIE. *(handing* **MABEL** *her gift.)* I got this in Jaffa.

MABEL. Your mailbox key is over on the counter. Sylvie, you didn't have to bring me anything.

(She opens up the box which contains earrings.)

Very nice! I'll wear them to the Senior Social this weekend. You're still coming with us, right?

SYLVIE. Actually, I forgot all about it.

MABEL. It's our annual bar-b-que. You have to come. I had the new girl at the front office put a ticket aside for you. We're all going in costume like we did last year. We had so much fun, remember?

FANNIE. Mabel's cousin Herman is coming, Sylvie. All the way down from Long Branch.

MABEL. Fannie! That was supposed to be a secret! Can't you keep anything to yourself?

FANNIE. But you said…

MABEL. Never mind what I said!

SYLVIE. Mabel, for the last time I am *not* interested in meeting your cousin Herman.

MABEL. Now, Sylvie…

SYLVIE. No, Mabel. I mean it. I won't go to the social if you insist on matchmaking. I still haven't gotten over my blind date with your podiatrist. He took me to dinner then spent the rest of the night clipping my toenails and examining my bunions. I wanted to die of embarrassment.

MABEL. So Alvin's got a foot fetish. So what? It's not every first date you get a pedicure.

SYLVIE. Dare I remind you about my lunch at Seafood Emporium with your dentist?

MABEL. I know, I know.

THELMA. What happened?

SYLVIE. He laughed so hard at his own dumb joke that his dentures flew out of his mouth and landed kerplunk in my cup of Manhattan claim chowder which then splashed all over my new white sweater.

MABEL. I always admired his perfect teeth.

SYLVIE. They may be perfect but I can assure you, they're not his. And, last but not least, my blind date with your accountant, Stan Weiner? After we finished dessert he got out his calculator and...

MABEL. He didn't ask you to split the check with him, did he?

SYLVIE. No, but that's not the point.

MABEL. You've got to respect a man who is careful with his money. Besides, Stan is the kind of man who...

SYLVIE. Why don't you fix up Fannie with your cousin? Or what about Rhoda?

THELMA. Hey! What am I, chopped liver?

SYLVIE. Thelma Wachter! You're married!

THELMA. So? Oscar's in Miami with his son until Labor Day. He'll never find out!

FANNIE. *(overjoyed with her big news)* I already have a date to the social!

SYLVIE. You do? Who?

FANNIE. Mabel fixed me up with Mr. Kastenberg in 515.

MABEL. Last year he went with Evelyn Greenbaum, but she's in rehab. You know, her little *"problem"* came back. *(mimics taking a drink)* She told me she was going down to Charleston for a couple of weeks but I'll wager dollars to donuts she's having a holiday at Betty Ford.

FANNIE. Mr. Kastenberg was so dashing in his sailor suit last year. Remember he won the prize for Best Male

Costume. The theme was "Seniors of the South Pacific." I wore a hula skirt and a pink lei. I think he liked watching me do the hula dance. Maybe this year he'll go as an Arabian Prince! And I'll be a belly dancer! This year's theme is "Seniors of the Sahara."

SYLVIE. That's so nice, Fannie. I'm sorry to hear about Evelyn, but I'm glad to hear about you and Mr. Kastenberg hitting it off. *(to* **MABEL***)* Why can't you introduce Herman to Rhoda? You know she's been after you to introduce her to someone.

MABEL. Rhoda isn't Herman's type. I'm a yenta, I *know* these things. I told Herman all about you, Sylvie. He wants to meet you.

SYLVIE. For the last time, *no thank you.* Honestly, aren't there any old ladies left in Long Branch?

MABEL. Well, I can't uninvite him. I hope you'll at least be civil.

SYLVIE. I'll be my usual charming self. But don't give him any wrong ideas. I'm not in the market for another fix up. Mabel, do you hear me?

MABEL. Oh, all right. You can't blame me for trying though. You two have so much in common!

SYLVIE. *(skeptically)* Like what?

MABEL. *(trying to think of something)* Well, he went over to Tel Aviv last March. For is grandson's bar mitzvah. I thought you could talk about your trip, and, well, who knows what else!

SYLVIE. Enough, Mabel! Subject closed. *(returning to the gift giving)* Thelma, thank you for driving me to the airport. I really appreciate it.

THELMA. I'm sorry you had to take a cab home. I don't drive at night anymore. I had a little accident.

SYLVIE. I know. I heard about Snowball. Poor kitty.

THELMA. I feel terrible.

SYLVIE. *(sympathetically)* It was an accident. Open your gift. I got this at the Eretz Museum.

THELMA. *(opening box containing a pin)* Ooooooh! I just love it Sylvie. Thank you for remembering me. *(She pins it* *on her blouse.)* Did you buy anything for yourself? Any souvenirs?

SYLVIE. I took a lot of photographs. I'm going to make an album of my trip. When I get them developed, I'll show you. Barry was *such* a handsome groom. And Rachel, what a *beautiful* bride! I cried through the whole ceremony. Oh, wait a minute! I did buy something else. Look at this. I bought it at an outdoor market when I went to Alexandria for the weekend with Rachel's aunt and uncle, Sidney and Phyllis. I couldn't resist it.

(She goes back into her suitcase and takes out a odd shaped teapot/watering can container.)

Isn't it wonderful?

THELMA. *(not too sure about what to say about the purchase)* What is it?

MABEL. It looks old. I mean, like an antique.

THELMA. It looks like a watering can.

FANNIE. It kind of reminds me of a tea kettle.

SYLVIE. I'm not sure exactly what it is. I couldn't really understand the woman who sold it to me.

MABEL. *(attempting to be politically correct)* Well, it's very nice. But, please don't ask me to swap it for my earrings.

SYLVIE. I know you think it's silly. But, I like it. I saw it and I knew I had to have it even though I know probably paid too much. I saw these things at the airport for half the price I paid.

MABEL. How much did you pay? Don't tell me! How much?

SYLVIE. *(picking up the "object" and admiring it)* About thirty dollars. But, I saw some just like this at the duty free stores in the airport terminal for half that price on my way home. I guess I got taken – or "ripped off" as my grandchildren say. But, I like this one the best. It's different somehow.

THELMA. You got it at an outdoor market? Did you have to barter for it? Did you have to trade anything? A ring or something?

MABEL. *(horrified)* I hope not.

SYLVIE. Oh no. Most of the stalls accept credit cards now.

MABEL. *(still unsure of the purchase)* What are you going to do with it?

SYLVIE. I'm not sure. Put it on my night table maybe. Or my dresser. I might even keep it on the table in here. As a "conversation piece."

(She places the "object" on the coffee table.)

MABEL. *(finally giving up the pretense)* Well, it leaves me speechless. But, so long as you like it, that's all that matters. Welcome home, Sylvie. We missed you.

SYLVIE. I missed all of you too. It's nice to be home again with my good friends.

MABEL. Come along gals. The world traveler needs some rest. Let me know if you want to ride the jitney with me to the shopping plaza to get your pictures developed tomorrow. I want to get us some do-dads from the party store for the senior social. I thought we'd all dress up harem girls this year.

FANNIE. I'm going as a belly dancer.

THELMA. Last year's social was so much fun. The ball game was on so Oscar pretended to have a headache and didn't go, remember?

FANNIE. Oh right! You hula danced the night away with Barney Finkelstein just to spite Oscar.

THELMA. I sure did. That is, until Barney's artificial knee gave way and the ambulance came. *(hugs **SYLVIE**)* Good night Sylvie. Don't forget to lock up.

SYLVIE. I won't. You too!

MABEL. We'll be fine. Come along, Thelma. Fannie and I will walk you to your apartment and see that you get in safe. Then we'll ride up to the the 5th floor together since we're just across the hall.

THELMA. Thanks Mabel. Good night Sylvie. Welcome home.

SYLVIE. I'll call you tomorrow!

*(**FANNIE**, **MABEL** and **THELMA** leave and **SYLVIE** locks the door and puts on the chain lock. She clears the coffee cups from the table and returns to look at "the object." The phone rings, it startles her as she is still "jumpy" from the break in, and she places "the object" on the end*

*table, near the edge, where it can easily topple over. She
goes to answer the phone.)*

Hello? Hello? Is anyone there?

*(No reply; she hangs up. She goes to the window and
looks outside. She makes sure it is locked. She goes to the
door to check the lock and make sure the chain is secure.
She puts a chair or small table in front of the door.)*

(to herself) I pay to live in a building with security and I
still get robbed. What is the world coming to?

(SYLVIE *rezips her small suitcase from which she retrieved
the presents and takes it and "the object" into her bedroom. She yawns.)*

Time for bed.

(There is a knock on the door.)

SAVALAS. Mrs. Goldberg?

(SYLVIE *enters the living room.)*

SYLVIE. *(goes to door but does not open it)* Who's there?

SAVALAS. Mrs. Goldberg, I am Detective Savalas with the
police. I need to speak with you about the events of
this evening.

SYLVIE. I'm afraid I'm very tired, Detective. Can't this wait
until tomorrow? I've already told the officers everything I know, which isn't all that much.

SAVALAS. I am sorry, no madam. This cannot wait. Your
cooperation is of utmost importance.

SYLVIE. Detective...I'm sorry what did you say your name
is?

SAVALAS. Savalas, madam.

SYLVIE. Savalas? *(thinks, then)* Like, that television detective?
Kojac?

SAVALAS. Yes, madam. Savalas, like the man on television. I
am Greek, as is he.

SYLVIE. You do have an accent, Detective.

SAVALAS. You are very observant, Mrs. Goldberg. I apologize if you are unable to understand me.

SYLVIE. Oh no. I understand you just fine. I just came home

from Israel where my grandson was married. I'm used to hearing accents like yours.

SAVALAS. I am glad.

SYLVIE. How do you like it here in America, Detective? I loved Israel but I don't think I could live there. I'd get homesick.

SAVALAS. I have been a proud citizen of the United States for more than twenty years. But, you are correct once again, Mrs. Goldberg. I do get home sick sometimes.

SYLVIE. *(sympathetically)* I'm sure you do. That's only natural. I was glad to get home and I was only gone for three weeks.

SAVALAS. Please, may I enter to speak with you? I know it is late. I won't take much of your time. My dear wife is waiting for me to come home.

SYLVIE. I'm sorry, Detective, I am very tired. I don't have anything else to tell.

SAVALAS. *(becoming more determined)* Mrs. Goldberg, I believe we have captured the man who attempted to rob your apartment. We have a suspect in custody and can only hold him for a few hours unless we have more evidence. I have some photographs to show you. You saw his face did you not?

SYLVIE. Only for a very brief moment. I don't think I would remember it. I hope you don't need me to identify him in a lineup!

SAVALAS. That will not be necessary. Please permit me to show you one or two photographs. Then, I promise I will leave.

SYLVIE. Oh, all right.

(SYLVIE unchains the door. As she opens it and SAVALAS enters she remembers to ask the "important" question.)

Oh, Detective Savalas, can you please show me your identification. You know, one can't be too careful.

(SAVALAS closes the door, puts on the chain and reaches into his coat pocket for his "badge.")

SAVALAS. You are correct once again, Mrs. Goldberg. You cannot be too cautious.

(Instead he pulls out a knife. SYLVIE gasps.)

Sit down. Do not scream. If you cooperate I will not kill you.

SYLVIE. *(woozy)* I'm think I'm going to faint.

(She grabs onto the back of the sofa)

SAVALAS. Do not do that, madam. I need to talk to you. Then I will leave.

(He escorts her around to the sofa and helps her to sit down.)

SYLVIE. What do you want with me? Are you going to kill me? That's not fair. I trusted you! You sounded like a real police Detective! Like Kojac! *(admonishing)* You should be *ashamed* of yourself.

SAVALAS. *(kneeling on the floor beside her)* When you were abroad, you purchased something. Something very valuable. Where is it?

SYLVIE. Valuable? I bought some gifts but I wouldn't say they were valuable. They were nice but quite inexpensive. I didn't even have to declare them at Customs.

SAVALAS. *(sternly)* I do not care about *trinkets*! I am talking about an *object*. A priceless treasure. A relic!

SYLVIE. A treasure? I live on a fixed income. I couldn't afford to go overboard on souvenirs. Plus, I could only fit so much extra in my suitcase. I only went over to see my grandson get married. I flew economy class! I can show you my boarding pass.

SAVALAS. *(losing patience)* We can do this the easy way or the hard way, Mrs. Goldberg. It is up to you.

SYLVIE. Can you please put the knife away? That would make it easier for me.

SAVALAS. If I do, will you cooperate freely?

SYLVIE. Do I have a choice?

SAVALAS. No.

SYLVIE. Then put the knife away. You said you wouldn't hurt me. So put it away. Then I'll believe that you are telling the truth.

SAVALAS. Very well. *(He returns the knife to his jacket pocket.)*

SYLVIE. That's much better. May I offer you a cup of tea or some coffee? I have some delicious cake in the kitchen.

SAVALAS. This is not a social call, Mrs. Goldberg.

SYLVIE. I'm just trying to be polite.

SAVALAS. I know you made a purchase at a stall in Alexandria.

SYLVIE. I did. Yes. But I didn't buy a treasure. I bought a teapot. It may be a watering can. I'm not quite sure what it is to be honest with you. It only cost about thirty dollars. It's probably just junk. I don't even know why I bought it. I got caught up in bustle of the outdoor market I guess. They sold them at the airport too.

SAVALAS. *(excited)* Where is it? Let me see it!

SYLVIE. It's drugs isn't it! I bet it's filled opium or heroin or crack cocaine. And I just sailed through Customs with it. How shameful! Are you a drug addict? I'll bet you need your fix.

SAVALAS. I am *not* a drug addict. I resent the implication.

SYLVIE. Then, you must be a drug pusher. A "King Pin." Isn't that what they're called?

SAVALAS. I am *not* a King Pin or a Drug Lord. I am not involved in drug trafficking. Mrs. Goldberg, this is the last time I will ask. Where is the object? I must have it now.

SYLVIE. All right. I'll get it.

(SYLVIE rises to go into her bedroom. SAVALAS starts to follow her.)

Please, wait here. I'd rather you not follow me into my bedroom. It's not proper.

SAVALAS. *(thinks for a moment, then)* Wait one moment. *(He goes to the phone and takes it off of the hook.)*
I will not follow you. But, do not anger me by trying to do anything foolish.

SYLVIE. Mr. Savalas, or whatever your real name is, I'm a retired school teacher. I'm not up to heroics. I'll be right back.

(She enters the bedroom, retrieves "the object" and returns with a spray bottle of household cleaner hidden behind her back.)

Is this what you are looking for?

*(As **SYLVIE** enters with the teapot, **SAVALAS** hangs up the phone, his eyes are wide and gleaming.)*

SAVALAS. Yes, that is it! Give it to me!

SYLVIE. With pleasure.

*(She crosses to him and to his surprise, sprays him in the face with" household cleaner" and then hits him over the head with "the object." Immediately as she does this he gives a loud cry "AAAGGH" and the strobe lights flicker for a few seconds. A harp plays in the background and a fog cloud appears all as part of "the genie effect." There is also trhe sound of a gong. She has broken "the object" and in doing so unleashes "EUGENE" from captivity from within "the object." She heads for the door, turns back to make sure **SAVALAS** is not following her. The lights stop flickering and **EUGENE** stands at the spot of the broken "object" ready to serve his new "mistress." **SYLVIE** stares at him dumbstruck as he has appeared out of nowhere. **EUGENE** is an "aged" genie, about the same age as **SYLVIE** and her friends. He wears the traditional "genie" outfit, harem pants, turban with broach and feather, vest, moccasins or bare feet.)*

EUGENE. *(with conviction)* Thank you, honorable mistress, for releasing me from the stronghold of the evil one's curse! I am humbly in your debt. I am faithfully at your service. I eagerly await the opportunity to pleasure your every whim. It is my duty to satisfy your every desire. It is my honor to obey your every command. *(He bows, then has trouble getting up and grabs the small of his back.)* ARGH! My lumbago.

*(**SYLVIE** faints at the door.)*

(BLACKOUT)

(The following morning. Lights come up. **SAVALAS***'s body has been removed from the living room. Sylvie is unconscious on the living room sofa, covered with a blanket, having been carried or dragged there by Eugene after she fainted.* **EUGENE** *has nodded off in the living room and waits for Sylvie to wake up. The phone rings a few times which startles* **EUGENE**.*)*

EUGENE. *(commanding, to the telephone which rings three times) (ring, ring)* Silence! You blasted contraption. Be silent! *(ring)* My mistress is at rest. You will disturb her slumber with your incessant clanging.

(The phone stops ringing.)

Such racket is enough to awaken the mummies in Pharaoh's tomb.

*(***SYLVIE*** awakens and stands up with a start. She sees* **EUGENE***, grabs the teapot, now broken, from the coffee table, ready to hit him.)*

SYLVIE. You! Get out! Now!

EUGENE. Good morning, fair mistress. Did you sleep well? I humbly apologize for the disturbance made by the clanging box. I have commanded it to be silent so as not to disrupt your much needed slumber.

*(***EUGENE*** bows to* **SYLVIE***, grabbing his back as he rises from the bow.)*

Owww. My sincere apology, mistress. I am unable to bow as deeply as in my early years.

SYLVIE. Stay back, I'm warning you. Don't come any closer!

EUGENE. You need not fear my presence, mistress. I trust that you have rested well. May I have the honor of preparing your morning meal? *(with a hopeful gleam in his eye)* Unless you wish me to see to your bath first, that is.

SYLVIE. Keep away from me! Don't you dare touch me. Are you a robber too? Am I being kidnapped?

EUGENE. You are quite safe. I am here to protect you. No harm will come to you now. You have my solemn promise.

SYLVIE. Who are you? What are you doing in my apartment? Where is the other man? The one who pretended to be a police detective?

EUGENE. I know of no detective. However, the villainous scoundrel whose head you used to free me from terminal bondage has been relocated to the small space which encapsulates your inclimate weather apparel.

SYLVIE. My what?

EUGENE. *(points to closet)* In there.

SYLVIE. He's in the closet?

EUGENE. Do not worry, he is quite incapacitated.

SYLVIE. He's dead? You killed him?

EUGENE. Not at all. *You* did when you bashed him in the head. I simply removed him from the center of the floor to a less conspicuous location. As I am no longer in my prime, I can assure you that it was no easy task.

SYLVIE. I have to call the police! *(She rushes to the phone and picks it up.)*

EUGENE. Perhaps. However, before you do please take a moment to ponder your present position. You will have to fully explain your actions and the authorities may not view them favorably in which case *you* may be forced to suffer the consequences.

SYLVIE. It was self defense!

EUGENE. Was he threatening you harm?

SYLVIE. Not exactly, but I think he would have. Besides, I didn't mean to kill him. I just meant to hurt him so I could get away.

(The phone rings again a few times.)

EUGENE. Please pardon my candor, mistress, but *that* annoying apparatus is an insult to my ears. It has bellowed several times this morning while you were deep in slumber from your ordeal of last evening and I cannot determine its purpose other than to startle one's unconscious and interrupt one's concentration. May I be so bold to inquire its purpose?

*(**EUGENE** grabs the small of his back and scrunches his face in pain and makes a groan of pain.)*

SYLVIE. What? It's a telephone! Who are you? What do you want from me? Why do you keep calling me "*mistress.*" *(slightly concerned)* And, what's wrong with your back?

EUGENE. Pay no consequence to my lumbago, mistress. I have endured the agony of the spine for many moons. As your servant, I must address you with the respect you deserve and recognize your authority notwithstanding that doing so may aggravate my deteriorating spinal condition.

SYLVIE. You're not my servant. I don't have servants. Get out of my apartment, now! Or, I'm calling the police.

EUGENE. I have nowhere to go, mistress. As your servant, I am dutifully bound to obey and attend you. Although, I must admit, this is the first time I have had the privilege to serve a member of your fair gender. My former masters have all been male.

SYLVIE. For the last time, who are you? Where did you come from? What do you want from me?

EUGENE. My name is Genesis Elijiah Nefarius Ivan Ethiopia, the Twelfth. To be sure, an elongated tryst for the tongue, which is why the former masters of my ancestry have shortened it to first initials, GENIE.

SYLVIE. Genie? *You're a genie?*

EUGENE. I am at that. Although, no longer in my prime, I have many good years ahead of me. I assure you, that by no means I have exhausted my usefulness of purpose.

SYLVIE. That's what Mabel always tells us when we complain about getting another year older.

EUGENE. Mabel gives sound advice, whoever she may be.

SYLVIE. Wait a minute. Wait just one minute! Mabel put you up to this, didn't she? You're cousin Herman from Long Branch! Mabel wanted to fix us up at the Social this Saturday and I told her I wasn't interested. Oh, no offense, Herman. I'm sure you're a nice man but I've had it up to here with Mabel's blind dates. My goodness, she just won't take no for an answer will she? I promised her I'd be civil to you but, really, I am not interested in any more blind dates, including you. Now, I hate to be rude but please leave.

EUGENE. I can assure you, mistress, that I have no affliction of the eyes nor am I related to a person called Mabel. However, I would be honored to escort you to whatever festivity you wish to attend.

SYLVIE. Sorry, the joke's over Herman. I'm just not interested. No offense but the last couple of times I went along with Mabel's matchmaking schemes I regretted it. Besides, don't you think you are taking this act of yours a little too far? Your get up is real convincing though. Is this your costume for the party?

EUGENE. I implore you to believe me, madam. I know of no Cousin Herman from Long Branch or anyone by the name of Mabel. And, although I have an ailing back I'm not blind. In fact, for a genie of my advanced age I'd have to say my vision is quite good. How may I prove to you that I am who I say I am?

SYLVIE. Okay, if you're a genie, then you must be magic, right? How about this? Since I've been traveling for the past three weeks I have no food in my refrigerator. Can you conjure up some breakfast? Say some eggs, toast, coffee and a V8, the tomato juice kind? Oh, go ahead, conjure up some breakfast for yourself too.

EUGENE. I would be delighted!

(He goes into the bathroom.)

SYLVIE. Uh, Herman – that's the bathroom. The kitchen's right there.

EUGENE. *(returning with tray of food, breakfast for two, including two small cans of V8 and a bottle of Vodka)*
I am sorry, mistress. I will learn to use the kitchen in the future. *(He sets down the tray of food.)* I hope this is to your liking. You did not specify if your eggs were to be scrambled, fried or over easy. I was not sure how you prefer your coffee so I left it black but brought you cream and sugar. I tasted the V8. It is quite delicious but I believe it would be even more so with a healthy splash of Vodka which I took the liberty to procure in the event that you agree with my observation. *(He pours the V8 into two glasses, one for himself and one for **SYLVIE**.)*

SYLVIE. *(in disbelief)* How did you do that? That's real food! *(She sits as if dazed.)* I fell and hit my head last night, didn't I. I have a concussion. I'm hallucinating. You're *not* real! That is *not* my breakfast. This isn't happening. I'm unconscious. I'm in a coma. I have a brain injury. I need medical attention. Call an ambulance!

EUGENE. Fear not. You are quite lucid. And, I am quite genuine. Although, if I may beg your indulgence, I am not at all certain as to who, exactly, you *are* or where, precisely, I *am.* I have the sense that I am no longer in the middle eastern part of the sphere.

SYLVIE. Are you telling me...do you honestly expect me to believe that you were in the...No. No! That's impossible. You're just a myth. There is no such thing as a Genie in a bottle.

EUGENE. I respectfully disagree.

SYLVIE. You are *not* a Genie! You did *not* simply spring to life when I smashed that tea pot over the detective's head. You went down to the coffee shop earlier, didn't you, and picked up the breakfast! The liquor store is right next door so I bet that's where you got the vodka. Unless you brought it with you.

EUGENE. Begging your pardon, mistress I did no such thing. I have not left your dwelling since I burst forth from captivity last evening. And, you have my sincerest appreciation for releasing me from the cramped confines that I have endured for more than *(thinks)* what year is this anyway?

SYLVIE. Oh, right. And, now what? You're going to tell me I have three wishes or some such nonsense? Do you think I was born yesterday? I don't know who you are or what you're trying to pull but the joke's over mister. Now get your geriatric genie bad back out of my apartment or I'll bash *you* over the head. *(She goes after him with the teapot.)*

EUGENE. *(backing away)* I beseech you, mistress. Please be kind, I am a genie of advanced age and am unable to heal from punishing strikes as in my younger servitude. *(He is still holding his back.)*

SYLVIE. *(regaining composure)* I'm sorry. I apologize. I won't hurt you. But, you have to promise not to hurt me either. I'm not used to waking up to a strange man in my apartment, not to mention a dead one in the closet. Sit down. Just sit down and don't move. I'll get you some ibuprofen.

EUGENE. *(sitting)* Thank you for your compassion and kindness, mistress. I am ashamed to admit that being confined to exceedingly cramped quarters for countless moons has adversely affected my formerly flexible physicality.

SYLVIE. Cut the crap, wiseguy. Do you really expect me to believe that you actually lived in a tea kettle for hundreds or thousands of years?

EUGENE. I tell you the truth, mistress. What you believe, however, is up to you.

SYLVIE. *(returning with the tablets and a glass of water)* Here. Take these. They're extra strength. They should kick in in about an hour.

EUGENE. *(skeptically)* Please forgive me, mistress, if I have in any way offended your sensibility. But before I take the poison pills you have proffered, I humbly beg you for your reconsideration.

SYLVIE. What? This isn't poison. It's ibuprofen. For your back pain.

EUGENE. I-bend-over-pro-friend?

SYLVIE. You've never heard of ibuprofen?

EUGENE. I have not. But, remember, I have been void of external communication for quite some time.

SYLVIE. Don't you watch television? All the medicine commercials?

EUGENE. *(examining the pills)* These small pods contain a potion for back pain?

SYLVIE. Yes, and other pain as well. Take two, you'll feel better. But they won't last long. If your back hurts that much you'll probably need to take more in a few hours. Just don't take too many in one day, or more than two at a time, three at the most.

EUGENE. *(swallowing the pills)* Once again, I am in your debt.

SYLVIE. If you are telling the truth...and...I can't believe I'm even considering the possibility...but, if you are telling the truth, what on earth am I to do with you? And, what about the man in the closet?

(The phone rings again.)

EUGENE. Silence, blast you!

SYLVIE. It's okay. It's okay. It's just a telephone...a communication device. I need to get this. Just sit here and be quiet. Please?

EUGENE. Your wish is my command.

(answering phone. during **SYLVIE**'s *conversation,* **EUGENE** *is mesmerized and awed by the phone and touches it.* **SYLVIE** *slaps away his hand.)*

SYLVIE. Hello? Good morning, Thelma. No, that's fine. You didn't wake me. You called earlier? I was here – uh, that is, I went downstairs to get a newspaper. Oh yes, I was up early this morning. No, I feel fine. I slept like a log. Lunch? *(She looks at* **EUGENE.***)* Well, uh, not today, I'm sorry. I've got a lot of unpacking to do and I want to get to the grocery store. Yes, I'll remember to get my ticket for the social before the front office closes. No, that's fine. You and Fannie go ahead without me. Have fun. Bye now.

EUGENE. It is clear that I have some competition in serving you mistress.

SYLVIE. What are you talking about?

EUGENE. You have another servant in your ringing box. I now understand its purpose. Undoubtedly, it is the sound made by another of your servants wishing to be released so that they may serve and obey. And you led me to believe that you doubted my authenticity. I suspect, to determine if I was worthy of being in your command. I hope that I have succeeded in passing your test.

SYLVIE. I'm sorry but I have no idea what you mean.

EUGENE. The ringing box! You were conversing with it! It must contain other of your genies. *(feelings hurt)* I was foolhardy to believe that I was to be the only genie in your life.

SYLVIE. This a telephone! Just a telephone. A way of talking to someone who isn't here. Where have you been for the last…oh, never mind.

EUGENE. Ah! I now understand! It is a device in which you conjure up ghosts and spirits! You then must be a witch? A sorceress?

SYLVIE. No! Of course not. I'm a retired school teacher. A telephone is used for communication. For talking to my neighbors on the 5th floor. Or, calling my grandson, Barry, in Israel, on weekends after 5:00 when the international calling rates are lower. Why am I explaining this? Oh, you're good. You're *very* good. A great actor is what you are. I just don't know what it is that you want from me.

EUGENE. I'm here to serve you, of course. And, to ensure that your life's pleasures are well attended. *(He groans and holds his lower back in pain.)*

SYLVIE. Ha! Not with your back the way it is.

EUGENE. *(innocently)* I beg your pardon?

SYLVIE. Nothing. That is, you don't exactly frighten me anymore. I mean I'm not afraid for my welfare. But, I'm not entirely sure what you mean or what I'm supposed to do with you.

EUGENE. Let me explain. What is it that you desire, wish for?

SYLVIE. Not the "three wishes" mumbo jumbo. I don't buy it.

EUGENE. Not three wishes! Not three hundred or three thousand! Your desires are limitless as is my ability to accommodate them. You asked me for breakfast and I provided it for you. Surely eggs and bread are not all that you want. What else do you desire? Property? Wealth? Revenge? Fame? Fortune? I can ensure that all of your worldly desires of grandeur are realized. That is why, I presume, that the villain in your cubbyhole sought to relieve me from your possession. My value is priceless as I am the last remaining Genie on the face of the earth.

SYLVIE. If you are so all powerful then how come you can't cure your own bad back? Huh? Answer me that one Mr. Magician.

EUGENE. Mistress, there some things even a genie is unable to do.

SYLVIE. Is that so? Like what.

EUGENE. We are unable to perpetuate eternal youth, eternal life or an existence free from disease or natural decomposition brought about by aging. If that were so there would be people walking around who are hundreds and thousands of years old which in turn would upset the coconut cart of existence. What we can do is to make one's life all the more pleasurable during the process of living.

SYLVIE. I can't believe I'm listening to this.

EUGENE. May I suggest, mistress, that you eat your breakfast before it turns cold.

SYLVIE. I'm not hungry anymore. You eat it.

EUGENE. Why thank you, I shall.

(*He eats.*)

SYLVIE. What if I wish you to go away and leave me alone? Would that count? Could you do that? First though, I would need you to help me do something to get rid of the man in the closet. I can't just leave him there. Too bad there's not a lake nearby.

EUGENE. You are a completely unique and unusual mistress. Never before has one of my captors released me from servitude with just two wishes fulfilled, one of them being a breakfast that you did not even eat. As to the man in the closet, if you wish him to be displaced, than displaced he shall be.

(**EUGENE** *enters the closet.*)

SYLVIE. *(shouting to the closet door)* That settles it. After you get him out of there I wish you your freedom if you promise you'll stay out of my apartment and leave me alone.

(doorbell rings)

Oh no!

(goes to door)

Who's there?

MABEL. Sylvie, it's me, Mabel. Who are you talking to? Who's there with you?

SYLVIE. Nobody! It's nothing Mabel. I'm fine. It's just the radio.

MABEL. You sound funny. What's wrong? Let me in.

SYLVIE. Ah, Mabel, I'm not feeling very well, I ah, I'll call you later, okay?

MABEL. You don't sound well, Sylvie. Let me in so I know you're all right.

SYLVIE. Mabel, it's not a good time, really.

MABEL. Did the robber come back? Is he holding you at gunpoint? That's it! I'm calling the police.

SYLVIE. No! No, don't do that, Mabel. I'm fine, really. I'll open the door. One moment, please. Let me just throw on some clothes.

(hurries to closet door, speaks to **EUGENE** *who is still in the closet)*

Stay put. Don't come out. Just stay in there until I tell you that it's okay to come out! *(to front door)*

*(***MABEL** *knocks loudly on the door.)*

Coming! Here I come!

*(***SYLVIE** *opens door,* **MABEL** *enters.)*

MABEL. What's going on in here, Sylvie? Who are you talking to?

SYLVIE. No one. Really, it was the radio. I'm sorry, I just don't feel one hundred percent today. You know, I guess the jet lag hit me. *(trying to usher her back out)* I really think I need to go back to bed for a couple more hours. Then I'll be fine.

MABEL. Something's fishy here, Sylvie. What are you trying to hide? Are you sure you're okay?

*(**EUGENE** emerges from closet and as he speaks **MABEL**'s jaw hits the floor. She is both dumbstruck and delighted.)*

EUGENE. *(to **SYLVIE**)* It has been my honor to pleasure your desires, fair madam. I'm certain that for the rest of my days I'll never have the privilege of satisfying anyone as lovely or unpretentious as you.

MABEL. Sylvia Goldberg!

SYLVIE. Mabel, it's not what you think!

MABEL. I daresay! Than just what is it? Not that it's any of my business, mind you. But Sylvie, I'm *impressed!* *(to **EUGENE**)* I'm Mabel Millstein, one of Sylvie's *dearest* friends. And, who might you be?

EUGENE. I am…

SYLVIE. Mabel, this is…ah…this is…this is, my friend Gene, that is, Eugene. We met on one of the day tours I took after Barry's wedding. He just stopped by for a visit.

EUGENE. I am honored to make your acquaintance. *(bows)* Owww. *(to **SYLVIE**)* I may need more of that i-bend-over- pro-friend medication. I fear that this morning's activities have further injured my back.

MABEL. Well I'll be a virgin on vacation. *(She goes to the breakfast tray and picks up the can of V8 and the vodka.)* Look at all this! What did you put in his V8 Sylvie? Vodka or Viagra?

SYLVIE. Mabel, it's not what you think.

MABEL. No wonder you didn't want to go to the Senior Social with cousin Herman. Looks like *you* already *have* a date. *(eyeing **EUGENE**)* And your date comes with his own costume.

*(Screams and commotion are heard from outside. **MABEL** and **SYLVIE** run to window to look out.)*

MABEL. That sounds like Gertrude Goldblatt! I wonder what happened!

SYLVIE. I can't see. There are too many people down there.

MABEL. I'll go check.

(**MABEL** *runs out the front door to see what has happened.*)

SYLVIE. (*To* **EUGENE**) I told you to stay in the closet! Why didn't you stay put like I told you to? What kind of genie are you that you can't even follow a simple direction?

EUGENE. I am indeed sorry, former mistress. I did not hear you.

SYLVIE. How could you not have heard me? Are you hard of hearing too?

EUGENE. No, former mistress. I have perfect hearing.

SYLVIE. Then why didn't you stay in the closet when I asked you to? Now Mabel knows about you and that means in five minutes everyone else will know too.

EUGENE. I did not hear you because I was fulfilling your command to displace the body from your closet.

SYLVIE. What does that have to do with your hearing?

EUGENE. I was out of the range of your voice.

SYLVIE. You were in the closet.

EUGENE. No, former mistress. I had left by then I assure you. Otherwise I would have stayed put as you commanded.

SYLVIE. Left? What are you talking about? There's no other way out of the closet and I was standing here the whole time. (*She looks closely at* **EUGENE.**) Your clothes are wet! Why are your clothes wet?

(**MABEL** *returns in a dither.*)

MABEL. Sylvie! This is so exciting! Between last night and this morning there hasn't been this much excitement around here in years!

SYLVIE. Mabel, what is it? What happened?

MABEL. *(catching her breath)* There's a dead body in the swimming pool! A man with his head bashed in! The police are on their way!

(Police sirens are heard as **SYLVIE** *faints once again.)*

(BLACKOUT/CURTAIN)

End of Act I

ACT II

Scene I

(SETTING: The following Saturday mid morning at the poolside patio off of the Social Room of Jerome Gardens, Margate, New Jersey.)

(AT RISE: FANNIE and THELMA are sitting at an outdoor umbrella table having their coffee on the deck and playing a game of cards.)

FANNIE. I'm so disappointed!

THELMA. Cheer up, you'll still have a good time. At least it's not supposed to rain until tomorrow. We can have the bar-b-que out here tonight instead of inside.

FANNIE. It's just not fair. I've been looking forward to tonight for weeks. I've been practicing my belly dancing every day. *(She demonstrates.)* It's a lot harder than the hula dance, let me tell you. If I do it too soon after I eat I get a bad cramp in my stomach.

THELMA. I'm sure you'll win the dance contest again this year. With those hips, you're a hard one to beat.

FANNIE. Not if I don't have a dance partner I won't! *(changing subject)* When I saw that ambulance pull up front this morning, I just knew who it was coming for. He did this just to spite me.

THELMA. That's crazy. Why would he do that?

FANNIE. I think he got jealous when I told him about the new gentleman who rented the Freeman's condo through Labor Day and how authentic looking his costume is. He won the best costume prize last year and I bet he wanted to win again this year. So, he's doing this just for spite. Because he's a sore loser.

THELMA. Fannie, it's not Mr. Kastenberg's fault that his pacemaker went on the fritz.

FANNIE. Oh, yes it is. Those things don't last forever you know. He should have had a maintenance check six months ago, not wait until the darn thing gave out.

THELMA. Fannie, it's a pacemaker, not a Buick. Anyway, Mabel's cousin Herman is still coming. Get her to fix it so you sit next to him tonight at dinner. If you're not interested in him, you never know, I very well may be.

FANNIE. Don't be silly. You're flying down to Miami on Tuesday to spend the week with Oscar.

THELMA. Not if I have a half a good reason to stay here. Speaking of which, when did you meet the Freeman's new summer tenant? Any vital statistics yet?

FANNIE. Vital statistics?

THELMA. Of course! Is he married? Jewish? Over 70? Under 65? Missing teeth? Toupee? Hair weave? Disagreeable odors or visibly disgusting habits?

FANNIE. *(laughs)* You've been hanging around with Mabel too long. I just caught a glimpse of him on Freeman's balcony yesterday morning. He was drinking a Bloody Mary and wearing some sort of a Sultan costume. I guess that means he's planning to come to the Social. We can meet him tonight.

THELMA. Good idea. We'll introduce ourselves and welcome him to the building. If we like him, I'll bake a pudding cake and we'll drop it by his apartment tomorrow. He'll have to invite us in for coffee if he's got any manners.

(**MABEL** *enters and rushes over to meet them. She has on sunglasses, a bathing suit with cover-up and sandals and carries a beach bag with a towel.*)

MABEL. Oh good, there you are! You'll never guess! I have *Information*!

THELMA/FANNIE. *(concurrently)* What?/What is it?

MABEL. It's a secret!

FANNIE. Even better! Tell us.

MABEL. If I tell you have to swear not to repeat it!

FANNIE/THELMA. *(concurrently)* Of course!/My lips are sealed.

MABEL. Okay. This is so exciting!

FANNIE. What is it already?

MABEL. Guess!

THELMA. Not this again.

MABEL. Don't be a spoil sport. I play along when you have *Information.*

THELMA. Okay. What's the category?

MABEL. If I tell you, you'll guess for sure.

THELMA. If you want me to work for it I at least need a category. Those are the rules.

MABEL. All right, don't get so official. Let me think. *(thinks then)* Category: "Who's been sleeping in my bed?"

FANNIE. That's my favorite category!

THELMA. Let's see. Male bed or female bed. I'll guess… male bed.

MABEL. Nope.

THELMA. Huh. How about that. *Female* bed. That makes it interesting.

FANNIE. Friend or relative? I guess it's a relative of a friend. I know! Sam Werner's daughter-in-law. She's such a floozy.

MABEL. Nuh-uh. Not a relative.

THELMA. *(thinking)* Hmmm. Female, friend. Okay, red head, gray or bleach blond. Umm, I'll go with bleach blond. Ha! I know who it is!

MABEL. No, it's not Gloria Lichtenstein but that's a good guess.

THELMA. Darn, thought I had it.

FANNIE. I can't think of anyone…Wait! What about Gladys Rosenberger?

THELMA. Oh right! She got divorced last year from husband number four, remember?

MABEL. Gladys always has company in her bed so it wouldn't be a big deal. I'll give you a clue. *Not* a bleach blond.

THELMA. Really? Then how about…no, she's blond…I can't think of any redheads. Gray?

MABEL. Yep.

FANNIE. You? Mabel, is it you?

MABEL. Don't I wish! No it's *definitely* not me.

FANNIE. Well, if it's not you, and it's not Thelma…Thelma, it's not you right?

THELMA. Not until Oscar comes home, darn it.

FANNIE. So it's not Thelma, and it's *not* me…then…I guess Sylvie.

THELMA. Don't be ridiculous. I guess Elaine Packer.

MABEL. One of you is correct.

THELMA. No kidding? Elaine's got a boyfriend already? Are you sure? Her husband has only been dead, what is it, ten months now? Who is it? Did you set her up?

MABEL. *(sing songy)* I didn't say it was Elaine.

FANNIE/THELMA. *(concurrently)* IT'S SYLVIE???

MABEL. Bingo!

FANNIE. You're making this up. I don't believe it.

THELMA. I do. Her "prim and proper retired schoolteacher widow" routine is a bunch of crap. She's as horny as the rest of us.

FANNIE. Who is she sleeping with? Did she tell you?

MABEL. Well, not exactly.

THELMA. Then how do you know she's got a gentleman caller. I still don't believe it.

MABEL. I'll tell you but you *can't* repeat this! Sylvie mustn't know that I told you. When she's good and ready she'll tell you herself.

FANNIE. What did you do, Mabel? Walk in on them or something?

MABEL. Or something.

THELMA. You did not! You walked in on them while they were…Oh my goodness! Of course, she gave you a copy of her key!

FANNIE. Oh, the poor thing. Sylvie probably died of embarrassment!

MABEL. No, no! I didn't catch them in the act. But, I'm pretty sure I caught them right after. The man couldn't even stand up straight from all of the *exercise.*

THELMA. When? When did you catch them together? She just got back from Israel a couple of days ago.

MABEL. It was the morning that Gertrude Goldblatt found the dead body floating in the swimming pool.

THELMA. Oh, I forgot to tell you. It wasn't a dead body after all.

MABEL. What?

THELMA. Ralph Waterman told me that he heard one of the paramedics say that the body still had a pulse. Anyway, Fannie and I missed all that commotion. We had just gone over to the Tropicana for the lunch buffet. Remember, Fannie? We called Sylvie to see if she wanted to go but she said she was too busy to come with us.

MABEL. She was busy alright!

FANNIE. Who? Who is Sylvie seeing? How long has this been going on? She's been out of town for three weeks. That sneak! Did she have a boyfriend before she left and didn't tell us?

THELMA. Who is it, Mabel? Anyone we know? Who?

MABEL. You may have seen him around. He's the new kid on the block.

THELMA. For pity sake, Mabel, tell us!

MABEL. You know the Freemans went to Europe and their place was up for summer rental, right? Well, *he* just rented their condo through Labor Day.

FANNIE. *Him?* We were just talking about him before you got here.

MABEL. You met him already?

FANNIE. No, but I saw him on the Freeman's balcony. He was all dressed up for the party tonight.

THELMA. Look! Here comes Sylvie.

MABEL. Not a word! I mean it! Or you'll *never* get any more *Information* from me!

THELMA. Shhh. Here she comes.

    *(**SYLVIE** enters.)*

MABEL. *(as an afterthought, whispering)* And, I'll never speak to either of you again! *(greeting **SYLVIE**)* Sylvie! How are you feeling? You gave me such a scare the other morning when you fainted dead away. I hope you made a doctor's appointment.

SYLVIE. I'm fine! It was jet lag, *that's all.* Stop fussing over me.

FANNIE. I can make you some chicken soup, Sylvie. That'll help you to keep up your strength…ah…that is, if you *need* to keep up your strength for anything…that is…I mean if you need to be strong for any type of physical activity…ah…not that I think you need to *exercise* or anything…*(checks watch)* Oh my, look at the time! Come along, Thelma, water aerobics starts in 15 minutes. We have to put on our swimsuits. Bye Sylvie. Coming Mabel?

MABEL. I'll meet up with you at the pool.

THELMA. Bye, Sylvie. I'm glad you're feeling better. *(as they exit)* Keep her strength up for physical activity? Oh, that was smooth, Fannie. Real smooth.

FANNIE. Leave me alone. I got tongue tied. I didn't say anything wrong.

SYLVIE. *(after they leave)* You told them, didn't you?

MABEL. I have no idea what you're talking about.

SYLVIE. What did you say to them?

MABEL. Nothing. I got here right before you did.

SYLVIE. I don't believe you. What did you tell them, Mabel? I don't want any gossip flying around.

MABEL. Don't worry. Your secret is safe.

SYLVIE. I don't *have* a secret. *(mutters to herself)* At least not the one you think.

MABEL. Well I'll be. Looky who's coming out for some fresh air and sunshine. *(She whistles or makes an appropriate sound of observational appreciation.)*

SYLVIE. *(looking)* What? Oh no!

*(**EUGENE** enters. He is dressed in swim trunks, sandals, a Hawaiian or beach shirt and carries a towel and a bottle of water.)*

What are you doing here? I thought you went away. I granted you your *(catches herself as* **MABEL** *is present)*...what are you doing here? Why are you dressed like that?

MABEL. *(to* **EUGENE***)* Don't mind Sylvie. I think she prefers you undressed.

SYLVIE. Mabel! Stop it! *Please!*

MABEL. Well, I'm off to the pool. I think I'll leave you two alone. Nice to see you again...Eugene, isn't it?

EUGENE. Good day, Miss Mabel. Indeed, the pleasure of reacquaintance is all mine.

MABEL. See you tonight at the Social I hope! Ta ta!

EUGENE. I'm very pleased that we meet again, Mistress, ah, I mean, Mrs. Goldberg. Once again, I thank you for honoring your promise of my freedom. If there is anything I can ever do for you in return, if it is within my power, I shall be most honored to accommodate you.

SYLVIE. Don't you listen? I don't want anything from you! I keep telling you that!

EUGENE. Of all of my former masters, you are by far the most selfless. If I may be so bold, may I inquire why you did not retain me in your service to fulfill your unattained desires, fantasies or pleasures? No disrespect intended, but the meager breakfast you wished for was hardly worth the effort on either of our parts.

SYLVIE. *(She studies him.)* Okay, you want to know? I'll tell you. I go to bed each night and before I fall asleep I do one thing. I thank God for all of my blessings. I have a wonderful life, my health, my family and my friends. I'm blessed to have everything I really need and then some. Oh, don't get me wrong, I'm not rich. But I'm not poor either. Yes, I live on a fixed income but I get by with my pension and social security. The only thing I want at this point is to retain my reputation as a respectable widow and for you to leave me alone! *(looks around, then whispers)* Now I appreciate your help in getting rid of the body in my closet. But, I wished you your freedom. What are you still doing here?

EUGENE. You are a very wise woman indeed. So many of my former masters were not careful about what they wished for. Therefore, so many of their wishes brought them nothing but disappointment and distress.

SYLVIE. I figured that out when the body I wished out of my closet ended up in the swimming pool. Besides, what else would I wish for? Money? I learned long ago that money can't buy happiness.

EUGENE. Precisely! It is unfortunate how many people never learn that valuable lesson – or – learn it the hard way or too late to benefit from the acquired wisdom.

SYLVIE. Since you're a free genie now, why are you here? Why didn't you go back to wherever it is that aging genies live?

EUGENE. I believe I told you. I am the last in a long line of genies. And, although rare that my ancestors were granted their freedom, as you so generously have granted mine, those that were have lived anywhere they chose. I have determined that I am quite satisfied right here. In Marge Ate Jew Nersey.

SYLVIE. Here? In New Jersey? You're going to live in *Margate?*

EUGENE. I am indeed, Mrs. Goldberg. In fact, my new residence, at least temporarily, is right up there *(He points.)* Dwelling number 808.

SYLVIE. You rented the Freeman's condo? How could you do this to me?

EUGENE. I simply made an inquiry about vacancies with the front office and was fortunate to have found the perfect abode. The staff in this building are quite accommodating.

SYLVIE. Didn't they do a background check? You're a genie! Do you have credit? A social security card? A green card? Do they *know what you are?*

EUGENE. The young woman in the office was of great help with completion of the paperwork. Of course, she very much appreciated the small bag of gold coins in exchange for her assistance. Also, she was quite pleased with the diamond and emerald earrings.

SYLVIE. Oh brother! The front office is on the take. No wonder the building got robbed.

EUGENE. To be sure, this is a very hospitable environment! Tonight there is even a festival in celebration of my heritage. "Seniors of the Sahara." I would be honored if you would accompany me to what is sure to be an entertaining and enchanting evening. *(He points to the sun as he does not wear a watch.)* I see that the sun is now high in the sky. Please pardon my hasty departure. Water aerobics is about to begin! *(as he exits)* I must learn how to interpret the sun dials that are common-place with the residents of Marge Ate. You know, like the one you wear on your wrist. *(He points to* **SYLVIE***'s wrist watch.)*

SYLVIE. *(to herself)* Why me? Why me? Why did I have to go to Alexandria for the weekend? Why did I have to buy that stupid tea pot? *(realizes where he's going)* Water aerobics? Oh no! They'll be all over him like cream cheese on a bagel. Wait! Eugene! Wait!

(She runs after him.)

(BLACKOUT/CURTAIN)

Scene II

(SETTING: The same except that it is now later in the evening and the party is in progress. The patio is decorated with a banner that says "Seniors of the Sahara" and there are balloons, twinkle lights and theme party decorations.)

(AT RISE: MABEL, SYLVIE, FANNIE, THELMA, EUGENE and HERMAN are sitting around a table. There are several cans of V8 vegetable juice on the table and a bottle of vodka. They are all "in costume" including EUGENE who is dressed as he first appeared as a genie. HERMAN wears a short sleeve shirt with a bow tie and a pair of suspenders to hold up his harem pants. He also wears white socks and shoes that lace. Fannie's belly dancing costume is the most elaborate of the womens.)

(With curtain closed, slow romantic music begins to play.)

MASTER OF CEREMONIES. And now, Seniors of the Sahara, here is some romantic music that will melt your heart if your sweetie hasn't already on this sultry summer evening at the New Jersey seashore.

(Curtain opens. SYLVIE, EUGENE, MABEL, FANNIE, THELMA and HERMAN are sitting around the table around at which they have just had their dinner by the outside poolside patio.)

MABEL. Herman, Fannie looks like she wants to dance. Why don't you ask her?

HERMAN. I'm sorry. I don't dance very well.

MABEL. It doesn't matter, Herman. Ask Fannie to dance. Go ahead. Fannie wants to dance, don't you Fannie.

FANNIE. That's okay, Mabel. We can sit here.

MABEL. Don't be ridiculous. You know you want to dance. Herman, dance with Fannie.

HERMAN. Fannie, would you like to dance?

FANNIE. Why, Herman, I would love to. Thank you for asking.

(FANNIE and HERMAN get up and start to dance.)

MABEL. Eugene, Sylvie looks like she wants to dance too.

SYLVIE. Mabel, stop it right now.

MABEL. You've been sitting there all night. I know you want to dance.

THELMA. C'mon. I'll dance with you Sylvie.

(THELMA begins to stand and MABEL pulls her back down into her chair.)

MABEL. No you won't! Eugene will dance with Sylvie, won't you Eugene?

EUGENE. Mrs. Goldberg, may I have the pleasure of dancing with you to this exquisite music?

SYLVIE. No. No thank you, Eugene. I'd rather just sit here.

MABEL. Don't listen to her, Eugene. Sylvie loves to dance. Don't you Sylvie?

SYLVIE. Mabel!

MABEL. In fact, Sylvie loves to *slow* dance, especially to Frank Sinatra.

EUGENE. Oh, I see. In that case, perhaps she would prefer to dance with him.

MABEL. Now that would be tricky!

EUGENE. Why is that?

MABEL. Because he's dead!

EUGENE. How unfortunate.

MABEL. But YOU'RE here, Eugene. So go ahead and ask Sylvie to dance.

EUGENE. I have, Miss Mabel, but Mrs. Goldberg does not wish to.

MABEL. Yes she does. Trust me. Go ahead and ask her again.

FANNIE. Owww. Herman, that was my bad toe you just stepped on.

HERMAN. Sorry about that. I warned you I'm not a very good dancer.

FANNIE. You're doing just fine, Herman. Just watch out for my tootsies.

SYLVIE. Mabel, if you keep this up I'm leaving.

EUGENE. Mrs. Goldberg since your former dance partner, Hank Sinatra, has departed this life to dance among the golden pyramids in the sky.....

SYLVIE. All right! All right already. Let's dance.

*(**SYLVIE** and **EUGENE** get up to dance.)*

FANNIE. Herman! Watch where you put that hand!

HERMAN. Sorry about that! You told me to watch your tootsies.

FANNIE. Yes but not with your hands!

EUGENE. You dance like a graceful swan, Mrs. Goldberg.

SYLVIE. Thank you. You know, you're a pretty good dancer yourself.

EUGENE. You seem surprised.

SYLVIE. Well, yes I am a little.

EUGENE. That's because my spine no longer ails me. Thank you once again for sharing your pain pods with me.

SYLVIE. Ibuprofin.

EUGENE. Did you know I once instructed the dancers in Cleopatra's court?

SYLVIE. You don't say?

EUGENE. Yes, and I taught King Tut how to do the.....

FANNIE. Ooowch! Herman no pinching!

HERMAN. It was an accident! My fingers slipped.

FANNIE. Herman, you're just a dirty old man. I knew I'd like you!

SYLVIE. You were saying?

EUGENE. It's not important. What is important is that this is a beautiful evening and I'm most satisfied to be spending it with all of my new friends in my new home in Marge Ate, Jew Nersey.

SYLVIE. Eugene, I...I...

EUGENE. Yes Mrs. Goldberg?

SYLVIE. Ah, I think I'd like to sit down now.

EUGENE. Of course. Thank you again, Mrs. Goldberg, for the delightful dance.

(**SYLVIE** *and* **EUGENE** *start to sit down at the table,* **FANNIE** *and* **HERMAN** *remain dancing as the music fades as the Master of Ceremonies starts to speak.*)

MASTER OF CEREMONIES. And now, for this evening's final contestant in the belly dancing competition, it is my pleasure to present Margate New Jersey's own Queen of the Nile, FANNIE GREEN!

(**MABEL, THELMA, SYLVIE, EUGENE** *and* **HERMAN** *cheer wildly as* **FANNIE** *gets up to dance. Middle Eastern "belly dancing" music starts and* **FANNIE** *gives it her all.* **HERMAN**'s *eyes bulge with excitement and desire as she dances around him and takes off scarves and runs them across his face and head as she is dancing. [She wears an age appropriate costume so that no "belly" actually shows.] She may even have a long colorful stuffed snake that she plays with as she is dancing. While dancing, she can move* **HERMAN** *and his chair center stage and give him a [rated G for geriatric] lap dance of sorts.* **HERMAN** *is enthralled with* **FANNIE** *and the women are in hysterics at their friend's spectacular performance and cheer her on.* **HERMAN** *and* **EUGENE** *are agog. After* **FANNIE** *is finished, they all rise and applaud her as" the crowd" goes wild with delight.*)

FANNIE. (*Gasping for air and flopping down in her chair*) WATER! I NEED WATER!

(**HERMAN** *pours her a glass from a pitcher on the table and* **FANNIE** *drinks it in a single gulp.*)

MORE!

(**HERMAN** *refills her glass and she drinks that too.*)

SYLVIE. Fannie! You outdid yourself! You were fantastic!

THELMA. You're sure to take first prize! Way to go, sister!

MABEL. Fannie, I've got to admit, you really know how to shake that booty of yours. You could charge for lessons.

EUGENE. Even the pharaohs would approve, Mrs. Green. Congratulations on a spectacular performance.

HERMAN. *(who is now smitten with* **FANNIE***'s display of charm not to mention her hips)* WOWEE! That was something! Can I watch you do that again sometime?

FANNIE. *(Still breathing hard)* Sure thing, Herman. But first I need to work my hip back in its socket. Thelma, feel like carrying me to my apartment?

*(***FANNIE*** tries to get up but can't and* **THELMA** *lends assistance.)*

THELMA. Hmmm. This is definitely a two person job. I need your help Herman.

HERMAN. Certainly!

*(***HERMAN*** assists under* **FANNIE***'s one arm and* **THELMA** *under* **FANNIE***'s other arm and they lead her off stage limping with hip pain.)*

EUGENE. *(Always a gentleman, he rises from his chair as they lead* **FANNIE** *away.)* Mrs. Green! May I suggest that you consume two pods of a remarkable potion for back pain? It is an incredible remedy. Since I started taking it my back has never felt better! I would be happy to share my reserve with you. I procured it from the shaman across the street. It is called I-bend-over-pro-friend.

FANNIE. You bent over who? Where?

SYLVIE. He means ibuprophen. He bought it at Walgreens. I have some upstairs. I'll get it for you.

FANNIE. No, that's okay. I've got some Motrin in my medicine cabinet. You just sit here and enjoy the rest of the evening with Mabel and Eugene. *You* may need your *own* ibuprofen later on tonight. *(She winks at* **SYLVIE***.)*

(She limps off with assistance from **THELMA** *and* **HERMAN***.)*

MABEL. Sylvie, look! There's Evelyn Greenbaum! She's back awfully soon from her visit with Betty. Uh oh! She's already got a glass in her hand. I hope it's just water.

*(***MABEL*** rushes off to greet Evelyn.)*

MABEL. *(continued)* Evelyn! It's so nice to have you back dear! How are you feeling? How was Charleston?

SYLVIE. Eugene. I need to talk to you. I don't know how to say this. I don't want you to take it the wrong way.

EUGENE. Speak your mind, Mrs. Goldberg. You won't offend me. Likewise, I hope I have not in any way offended you.

SYLVIE. No, of course not. Please, call me Sylvie. Everyone else does. Mrs. Goldberg is so formal.

EUGENE. Of course. Sylvie is a lovely name. And certainly fitting, as you are a lovely woman. What is it you wish to tell me, Sylvie?

SYLVIE. Eugene, I'm happy that you are having a good time here.

EUGENE. Oh, I am, Sylvie. I am. Marge Ate Jew Nersey is a magnificent metropolis.

SYLVIE. And, I'm very glad that you've made new friends.

EUGENE. Extraordinary human beings! I fully appreciate why you feel blessed.

SYLVIE. But…

EUGENE. Yes? Go on.

SYLVIE. This is the hard part, don't rush me.

EUGENE. I apologize. Please take your time.

SYLVIE. I was worried that you would blow your cover. And, you haven't. I'm very grateful for that.

EUGENE. Blow my cover? I do not understand. You worried that I would subject your friends to some sort of sordid depravity?

SYLVIE. No, no! Nothing of the kind. "Blow your cover" means…ah.. it means let on…let people know, by mistake or even on purpose, that you are a genie. That you came back with me from Israel in a tea pot.

EUGENE. You are mistaken, Sylvie. I was not in Israel. I was in Egypt.

SYLVIE. Yes, I know. I went there for the weekend to sightsee when I was in Israel to see my grandson get married.

I actually took you – your canister – or tea pot – whatever it was you called home for all those years – back with me to Israel for a week before I – we- flew home.

EUGENE. We *flew* home? On a magic carpet?

SYLVIE. No! On an airplane! See, that's just what I'm talking about. That's what scares me.

EUGENE. I can understand that! Flying on top of an aeroplane must be terrifying! I believe I saw quite a few of them this afternoon while I was at the beach. Aren't they the large bird like creatures that fly over the ocean with long tails that say "All you can eat lunch buffet for nine ninety nine."

SYLVIE. Yes. No! Flying in an airplane doesn't scare me. Air travel is safer than driving a car. Just ask Thelma.

EUGENE. Then, I don't comprehend.

SYLVIE. What I mean is, there are so many things that are different, here in Margate, New Jersey, than where you come from. Let's face it, you were cooped up in that tea kettle for a long long time.

EUGENE. Tell me about it!

SYLVIE. And, there are so many things that you say and do that make you "different" from the rest of us. You could easily "blow your cover" for lack of better words. And that would be awful. Just awful. For both of us. At least one person already knows that I bought you and brought you back with me. He broke into my apartment to get you back – and my friends and I could have been hurt or even killed.

EUGENE. Yes, that was quite unfortunate.

SYLVIE. And, I killed him. In my whole life, I've never killed a bug, Eugene. Yet I killed that man. I didn't mean to. I was very afraid and I do believe I did it in self defense. But, he's dead and it's my fault. And, I didn't do the right thing, Eugene. I should have called the police but I didn't. And the reason I didn't is because I didn't know how to explain you or why the man broke in or what he was trying to find. I don't know how I'll live with myself for that. But, I can't go to the police now. They would never believe me. How would I have gotten him in the pool? I'd have to tell them about you. And, I couldn't do that to you. Your life would be ruined if people found out what you are. It's better just left alone. But, I do feel terrible in the pit of my stomach, for taking someone's life. Even if it was an accident. I really didn't mean to kill him. I just wanted to hurt him so I could get away.

EUGENE. Are you telling me you want me to go? To leave Marge Ate? Forever?

SYLVIE. I'm sorry, Eugene. I'm very sorry. I like you. I really do. We all do. Mabel and Fannie and Thelma. Even Herman. He's not such a bad guy after all. He and Fannie really hit it off, didn't they?

EUGENE. It appears as though they have.

SYLVIE. If you stay here, even if you don't blow your cover, every time I see you I'd remember that horrible night and what I did. And, Eugene, that is something that I'll never be able to put behind me. But, if I saw you every day, or even a few times a week, which would probably be unavoidable, I'd have a very hard time. Margate is not a metropolis, Eugene. It is a very small town.

(EUGENE rises and bows.)

EUGENE. I wish you no discontent, Sylvie. I only wish you joy and happiness. As it is joy and happiness that you have brought to me. You are a very special lady. I am glad to have met you. And, I will always be grateful for your grant of my freedom so that I may live out the rest of my years without oppression or in captivity. Now, I bid you farewell and good fortune. *(He takes her hand and kisses it.)* Please tell our mutual friends that I was happy to have made their acquaintance and that I shall miss them. It is you, however, I will miss most of all. Goodbye, Sylvie Goldberg.

SYLVIE. Thank you, Eugene. Safe travels to you. *(after EUGENE exits)* I'll miss you too.

(**FANNIE** *and* **THELMA** *rush back.* **FANNIE** *is still limping but full of excitement.*)

FANNIE. Sylvie! Sylvie!

SYLVIE. What? What's wrong? Where's Herman?

THELMA. He's upstairs, standing guard.

SYLVIE. Standing guard? For what?

THELMA. Fannie didn't have any Motrin in her apartment!

FANNIE. Actually I had some, but it expired.

SYLVIE. Okay, I'll go get mine.

FANNIE. No! We ran into Mabel talking to Evelyn Greenbaum and Mabel lent me your key to go get it myself. I hope you don't mind.

SYLVIE. No, that's fine. Did you find it? I keep it in the kitchen.

THELMA. No! When we got to your apartment your front door was ajar!

SYLVIE. That's impossible. I'm sure I locked it before I came down for the party.

FANNIE. Somebody broke in again Sylvie! They ransacked your apartment!

SYLVIE. What? Oh no! No one was there when you got there I hope? You're okay aren't you?

FANNIE. We're fine. We ran out pretty quick. Well, I limped out actually. But we didn't see anyone. I think they left. Herman's up there now in case they come back.

SYLVIE. He shouldn't be up there! What if they come back? He could get hurt.

FANNIE. He can protect himself. Herman's got a black belt in – what's it in again, Thelma?

SYLVIE. A black belt? Herman? Are you sure you don't mean black suspenders?

FANNIE. As a retired school teacher, Sylvia Goldberg, you ought to know by now to never judge a book by its cover. Herman is a real tiger. He was a Marine.

THELMA. Sylvie, you've got to go call the police. Why does somebody want your things? What do you have in there? The national treasure?

SYLVIE. Not anymore.

FANNIE. What?

SYLVIE. Nothing. Oh, this is terrible. I guess I do have to call the police.

FANNIE. Of course you do! Here, you can use my cell phone. *(She reaches into her costume and pulls out her phone and gives it to SYLVIE.)*

(MABEL returns.)

MABEL. I was right! Evelyn had more than water in that glass. Poor thing. Look at her. She can hardly stand up straight. What's going on?

THELMA. Sylvie's apartment got robbed again!

MABEL. Sylvie! What are you hiding in there? Besides, Eugene that is?

THELMA. Where *is* Eugene?

SYLVIE. Ah, he was tired and he went up to bed.

MABEL. I'm going to tell him. He'll want to know about this. *(She runs out to EUGENE's apartment.)*

SYLVIE. Mabel, no! Wait! Don't!

THELMA. Go, ahead. What are you waiting for? Call the police.

SYLVIE. I'm light headed all of a sudden. I have to sit down.

THELMA. Let me pour you some water. *(She pours from the pitcher which is now empty.)* Fannie finished it. I'll go get some more. I'll get you something stronger too. To calm your nerves. I'll be right back. *(She exits)*

FANNIE. Give me the phone. I'll call the police. *(FANNIE takes the cell phone.)* Darn, no signal. Maybe it'll work out front. *(She exits limping with the phone.)*

(After they have all gone, SAVALAS enters. He is dressed in full costume with his face covered. He approaches SYLVIE.)

SAVALAS. We meet once again Mrs. Goldberg. *(He takes out a knife.)* Do not make a scene. Please, come with me and you will not be hurt.

SYLVIE. It's you! I thought you were dead. I thought I killed you.

SAVALAS. You almost did. That was a splendid show of bravery for a retired school teacher. I required several stitches and suffered a small concussion. Shame on you for leaving me in your swimming pool to drown. Though, I cannot imagine how I got there. Your annoying friends helped you I suppose. I assure you I will not put away my knife while I am in your company this time.

SYLVIE. I'm sorry. I'm so sorry. I only meant to hurt you, not kill you. I'm glad you are not dead.

SAVALAS. Mrs. Goldberg, I assure you that if you do not cooperate with me this time you will in fact wish that you had killed me. Let's go. Now. I am not leaving without the treasure for which I came. And you are going to give it to me.

(entering)

EUGENE. *(enters carrying a golf club)* You are wrong, former master, if you don't unhand the lady at once, *I* am going to give it to you! *(He picks up the club as if to swing it at* **SAVALAS***'s.)*

SAVALAS. You! You have escaped from captivity! I command you to reenter confinement at once! *(He picks up an empty wine bottle from the table.)* Confinement! Now!

EUGENE. I am no longer under your control or at your service. I will repeat myself only once more. Unhand the lady now or you will sorely regret the day you ever enslaved me.

SAVALAS. So, she is your new master? This *woman*? This *Sylvia Goldberg* from Margate, New Jersey is the master from whom you now take your orders! Well, I can fix that. *(He puts the knife to* **SYLVIE***'s throat.)* You have one last wish, my lady. Do you know what that wish is? You will wish that your genie once again belongs to me. If you do not, I will kill you.

SYLVIE. But, I already…he's already…

EUGENE. Go ahead, mistress. *(He winks at* **SYLVIE.***)* I beg you to save your life. Make your final wish on this man's behalf.

SYLVIE. *(catching on)* I wish that you belonged to him again.

SAVALAS. *(tossing* **SYLVIE** *aside)* You heard her. Now you are mine once again! I command you to re-enter confinement.

(He holds the wine bottle out to **EUGENE.***)*

If you do so now I may be inclined to be somewhat lenient with your inevitable punishment. Say twenty lashes instead of thirty, old man?

EUGENE. Yes, master.

(He reaches for the wine bottle as if to pop into it but instead grabs it and hits **SAVALAS** *over the head and fights him to the floor where he sits over him with a chair and holds* **SAVALAS***'s knife at his neck.)*

SAVALAS. You insolent piece of rubbish! You have now earned one hundred lashes for your disobedience. How dare you. Let me up at once.

EUGENE. *(to* **SAVALAS***)* I forgot to tell you, former master, this lovely lady granted me my freedom. It was the second wish she made. Her first wish was breakfast for both us. Have you ever had a V8? It is quite tasty.

(Sirens are heard in the background.)

(to **SYLVIE***)* Fear not, Sylvia Goldberg, the police are on their way. It is not I who will spend time confined to captivity. It is you.

*(***EUGENE** *lets* **SAVALAS** *up, while continuing to hold the knife on him.)*

Let's go meet your new captors, shall we? I'm sure you'll be gratified to know that your reputation as the "pizza burglar of Marge Ate" precedes you.

(He leads **SAVALAS** *off.)*

*(***MABEL** *and* **THELMA** *rush back from different directions.* **THELMA** *carries a water pitcher and a bottle of vodka.)*

MABEL. Eugene wasn't there. I knocked and rang his door bell but he didn't answer. I hope he's not two-timing you, Sylvie.

THELMA. Here, Sylvie. Here's your water.

SYLVIE. Thanks.

(**SYLVIE** *instead grabs the bottle of vodka and drinks a big gulp.* **MABEL** *and* **THELMA** *look at each other quizzically as* **SYLVIE** *rarely drinks.*)

(**FANNIE** *runs in limping and panting out of breath.* **HERMAN** *is with her.*)

FANNIE. Eugene! The robber! Eugene! The robber? Outside! The police! They're arresting him!

MABEL. The police are arresting Eugene? He's the robber!

THELMA. I knew there was something different about him. I just couldn't put my finger on it.

FANNIE. No, Eugene *caught* the robber. The police arrested the robber, not Eugene. They're taking him away now. Eugene is a *hero*!

MASTER OF CEREMONIES. Attention Seniors of the Sahara! We're coming to the close of this magical evening and I hope that all of your wishes came true. Now, for the moment that you've all been waiting for! It's time to announce the prize winner of the final contest of the night. The prize for the best belly dancer goes to *(drum roll)* Margate's own Queen of the Nile, FANNIE GREEN! *(loud cymbal sound)* Come on over here Queen Fannie and claim your treasure!

(**FANNIE** *squeals with delight and plants a big kiss on* **HERMAN** *who is pleasantly surprised. Everyone shouts for approval and applauds and* **FANNIE** *limps off with the help of* **HERMAN**, **THELMA** *and* **MABEL** *to claim her prize.*)

(**EUGENE** *returns.*)

EUGENE. I'm very pleased by the outcome. Fannie deserved to win.

(**SYLVIE** *turns around to see him. She goes over to him*

and they embrace. She starts to cry.)

Everything will be fine now. My former **master** has been taken to jail. He will certainly be **deported**. You are safe now. He will never bother you **again**. **It** would serve him no purpose for he knows I am **emancipated**. He is of no future harm to either of us.

SYLVIE. Thank you. Thank you so much. You **saved** my life. I believe he really would have killed me this time.

EUGENE. You also saved mine. In more ways than one. I am glad that I could return the favor. Now, I will keep my promise to you. I will go now, Sylvie, and leave you to resume your life as you know it. *(He turns and starts to leave.)*

SYLVIE. Eugene, wait! Please, don't go!

EUGENE. But I must, Sylvie. I was on my way out the first time when I spied the evil one from across the room. I knew he was up to no good. I followed him to make sure you were safe. Not to cause you more distress.

SYLVIE. I know that. I changed my mind. I want you to stay. In Margate. With me. With all of us. Please? Please will you stay?

EUGENE. What about our differences? Our cultures? What would you do if I were to…what is the phrase? *(thinks)* "Blow my blanket?"

SYLVIE. I didn't realize how much I would miss you until after you left. I think that one of the reasons I'd miss you so much is because you *are* different. Being different isn't a bad thing. It's a good thing. With you, it's a wonderful thing. Please, Eugene. Please stay?

EUGENE. *(thinks)* I'll stay under one condition!

SYLVIE. What's that?

EUGENE. That you have breakfast with me tomorrow morning. And we share a V8.

SYLVIE. You're on!

(They hug then, of course, kiss.)

Eugene, not everything I told you earlier this evening was one hundred percent true.

EUGENE. It was not?

SYLVIE. I told you how happy I was. And I am for the most part. But I do get lonely sometimes. Oh, Mabel and Fannie and Thelma are wonderful friends but it's not the same as...

EUGENE. As what, Sylvie?

SYLVIE. I told you I didn't wish for anything. That isn't really true. It doesn't matter now, though. I think that the one thing I've been wishing for just came true.

(They kiss again as **HERMAN, FANNIE, THELMA** *and* **MABEL** *enter.)*

MABEL. What is this? The *senior* prom? Get a room you two!

HERMAN. Woo Hoo!

FANNIE. Sylvie's got a boyfriend! Sylvie's got a boyfriend!

THELMA. *(singing)* Sylvie and Eugene, sitting in a tree.

THELMA, FANNIE, MABEL & HERMAN. *(singing)* K-I-S-S-I-N-G.

HERMAN. That looks like fun. What do you say we give it a try?

*(***FANNIE** *and* **HERMAN** *kiss.)*

MASTER OF CEREMONIES. And, that concludes our evening of enchantment, Seniors of the Sahara. On behalf of building management, we hope everyone had a wonderful time. By popular demand, the theme for next year's bar-b-que will be "Seniors of the South Pole." Wait a second! Look! Up in the sky! Over the ocean! A falling star! Two, three – no – four of them! We may be having a meteor shower! Quickly, Seniors of the Sahara, *make your wishes*! But, be careful what you wish for! You never know, they just may come true!

*(***MABEL, THELMA, FANNIE** *and* **HERMAN** *look up in awe and point to the falling stars.* **EUGENE** *and* **SYLVIE** *kiss as the curtain closes and the lights fade.)*

End of Play

PROPERTY LIST

ACT 1

Prequel (To simulate a "far off land")

Stool for REFIK (optional)

Credit card receipt (REFIK)

Passport information written on piece of paper (REFIK)

Whip, riding crop or black pipe for Savalas to threaten REFIK.

Artificial tree in pot/stand with stuffed animal snake wrapped in the branches (optional)

Sylvie's condo

Welcome Home Sylvie sign

Scotch tape (on ledge in kitchen)

Balloons

Four coffee mugs

Four paper plates

Four Forks

Breakfast tray offstage in bathroom with: plate, scrambled egg, toast, coffee mug, cream, sugar, glass of V8

Bottle of Vodka for Eugene to carry on with breakfast tray

Water glass and white candy to simulate ibuprofin in kitchen

Suitcase containing gifts wrapped in tissue paper: pin in box, earrings in box, scarf in box and an *unusual looking teapot or watering can* with removable lid gently taped closed

Pizza box for Savalas to carry on

Pudding cake for Thelma to carry on

Lamp – turned ON.

Microphone for Salavas to talk into when he is talking to SYLVIE through her front door

Knife for SAVALAS to carry on to threaten SYLVIE. Cleaning solution bottle (washed thoroughly and filled with water)

Plants around SYLVIE's apartment for MABEL to compliment FANNIE's good job watering

Kitchen curtains or wall hanging visible from behind a half wall/counter

Bar stools or small table for 2 in front of the half wall/counter

Fog machine off stage (recommended for "genie effect" when Eugene springs to life from teapot)

Love seat

Chairs (2)

Sofa tables

Telephone

Coffee table

Note: Suitcase needs to be put on stage during the blackout following the "*SURPRISE*."

During intermission: Strike indoor furniture, set up the outdoor furniture and the outdoor artificial trees with white lights in the pots.

ACT 2

Scene 1

Deck of cards preset on table

Water bottle (Eugene optional)

Towel (Eugene)

Artificial trees with lights off

Outdoor table(s) and chairs and optional umbrella

Remove curtain from kitchen

To simulate an outdoor courtyard put signs on the doors of SYLVIE's apartment "Ladies Room" "Mens Room" "Wheelchair accessible" "Authorized Personnel Only"

Beachbag (MABEL)

Wristwatch (SYLVIE)

Scene 2

Turn on lights on the artificial trees

Flameless candles turned on around the set as would be appropriate at an outdoor party

Red plastic cups on table with water pitcher and cans of V8. Water pitcher should only contain a small amount of water – enough for 2 cups, small – it has to "run out"

Vodka bottle off stage for THELMA to carry on

Cell phone in FANNIE's costume – turned off

Wine bottle on the "other" (2nd table)

Knife for SAVALAS to threaten SYLVIE again (he carries this on)

Cordless microphone for Master of Ceremonies

Belly dancing trophy for FANNIE to carry on (optional)

Golf club (for EUGENE to carry on to threaten SAVALAS)

Head bandage (SAVALAS)

AUTHOR'S NOTE REGARDING "THE GENIE EFFECT" IN ACT 1

When Eugene is released from the teapot in Act 1, the release should be dramatic with respect to lighting and sound effects to include strobe lights, thunder, a harp, a gong and, if possible, a cloud of smoke/fog from a fog machine. After Sylvie hits Savalas with the pot, it should shake violently in her hand until she drops it.